Maizie Moc

MW00897404

a Dog Who is Blue

Stories by: Pamela E. Titus

Illustrations by: Ruby Biggs

DEDICATION

The Maizie Moo series is dedicated to not only adoptive dog families, but to blended families of all kind. May there be love, good family living and lessons in every day we co-exist. A special thanks to those who dedicate their love and lives to re-homing those in need. Maizie would like to thank some of her favorites including Best Friends Animal Sanctuary and particularly Vicky's Pet Connection for helping her find her forever home and as we, her family, like to say "where she hit the motherlode".

CONTENTS

ACKNOWLEDGMENTS

Special thanks to Maizie for allowing me to share her antics and one of a kind personality. A big thank you to Ruby Biggs, just a kid herself, for taking a risk and demonstrating her talent in expressing Maizie's sweetness in a book for kids. I wish her the best in her exploration of her creativity in the professional art world. Thanks to my friends and family, in particular my sister Karen who encouraged me to finish this project even when I struggled. I write so others will read, because it matters. Read everyone, read.

STORY ONE:
WELCOME HOME

I know you're adopted. I came the same way.
No need to be scared, it is your lucky day.

My name is Teeter. I'm black and you're blue.
Stick with me Maizie Moo you will learn what to do.

When friends come over and you need something to eat
Bark your fool head off and they will give you a treat.

The trash is a treasure, like hunting for prey.
Be careful I'll warn you, mom must be away!

When she comes home she'll yell: "Who made all this mess?"
Look up with your brown eyes: "The cat did, I guess?"

Bye-bye is a good word just listen for keys.
Can we go through the drive thru? Can we, pretty please?

In the car when mom's driving and you just want some air,
Paw right at the window it will open, I swear!

When the day is all over and it is time for some rest;
Jump up on mom's bed we will make us a nest.

You will sleep really well all snuggled in tight.
Mom will kiss you and hug you then tell you good night.

As I think of our day I may have taught some bad things.
You should listen to mom it is true love she brings.

STORY TWO:
PLAY DAY

Her head is black and her body is blue.
When she is happy or playing
she makes a sound that goes "MOO!"

She is a silly girl who likes to have fun.
Should we stay inside or go out in the sun?

Mom bought a toy chicken at the store last week.
It is fun to play with and it says, "SQUEAK, SQUEAK"!

The best of both worlds, take the chicken outside.
A pile of leaves, hurry, let's hide!

A bunny goes hopping and look, there are squirrels;
She will chase with her sister, they are such silly girls.

She will stop for a minute to smell pretty things.
She looks to the sky as a birdie sings.

Hey, there's the mailman! She gives him a "BARK".
Mom pulls her away and they head to the park.

Chasing sticks and balls, the park is such fun.
Let's rest for a while and soak up the sun.

When we get back home it is time for some lunch.
Mom gives her a bone, YUM, YUM, CRUNCH, CRUNCH.

So very tired, it is time for a nap.
She lies on the couch with her head on mom's lap.

She had so much fun. She made the most of her day.
She hopes you remember you should live the same way.

ABOUT THE AUTHOR

Pamela is a Communications major who tutored writing in college. Her love of storytelling to share a message drives her to write and publish books which do exactly that. Pamela considers the richness of the written word an art form to be shared for the young and the aging. Her ability to inspire others comes through in her daily living and she aspires to demonstrate that whether broken or downtrodden, everyone has something to give back to this earth and those who walk it and live together upon it.

35762811R00020

Made in the USA
Middletown, DE
14 October 2016